Rosie & Jim
and the Drink of Milk

Written by John Cunliffe
Illustrated by Celia Berridge

Based on the Central Independent Television Series produced by Ragdoll Productions

Hippo Books
Scholastic Children's Books
London

Scholastic Children's Books,
Scholastic Publications Ltd,
7-9 Pratt Street, London NW1 OAE, UK

Scholastic Inc.,
730 Broadway, New York, NY 10003, USA

Scholastic Canada Ltd,
123 Newkirk Road, Richmond Hill,
Ontario, Canada L4C 3G5

Ashton Scholastic Pty Ltd,
PO Box 579, Gosford, New South Wales,
Australia

Ashton Scholastic Ltd,
Private Bag 1, Penrose, Auckland,
New Zealand

First published by Andre Deutsch Children's Books 1992
An imprint of Scholastic Publications Ltd

This edition published by Scholastic Publications Ltd. 1993

ISBN 0 590 55082 9

Printed by Mateu Cromo, Madrid

Rosie and Jim are on their boat, the good boat Ragdoll.
John steers the boat. Rosie and Jim look out to see what they can see.
What will they find today for John to put in his book?

"Where are we going?" said Rosie.
Jim popped his head out of the window to have a look.
"John says we're going to the countryside," said Jim.
"Oooh, noggin," said Rosie. "Let me see."
Rosie popped her head out.
"No houses," she said. "No shops...not one."
"And lots of trees and grass," said Jim.
"And hills and sky," said Rosie.
"They have sky in the town," said Jim.
"But there's more of it here," said Rosie.
"Is this the countryside?" said Jim.
"That's what fuzzy-face said," said Rosie.
"They have milkmen," said Jim. "Look there's one, now."

They could hear John talking outside.
"That reminds me. I have some nice milk-shakes
in the fridge. It makes me feel quite thirsty."

"Me, too," said Rosie.
"And me," said Jim. "We could have...just...one..."

Rosie and Jim had a milk-shake each. They left one in the fridge for John.

When the boat stopped, John said, "This looks like a nice place for a walk."
Off he went, across the fields, with Rosie and Jim not far behind.

John stopped to look over a gate. Rosie and Jim peeped through a gap in the hedge.
"Oh, Rosie," said Jim. "There's a great big monster in there, with goggly eyes and a long lollopy tongue! There are lots of them."

All John said, was, "There's a nice field of cows. I bet they give a lot of milk."

"Oh, gobbin," said Rosie, "your monster's a cow. That's what John called it."

"A cow?" said Jim. "Will it gobble us up?"

"No," said Rosie, " look. It only wants to eat grass."

"Do you mean this stuff?" said Jim, with a bunch of green grass in his hand.

"That's right, noggin," said Rosie.

"But John said cows can give us milk," said Jim. "Where can they get it from, when there are no shops here?"
"How do I know?" said Rosie. "We'd better get a move on. Look, John's off again."

"There's a farm on the hill," said John. "I wonder if I could get a drink of milk there? I'm so thirsty…"
John knocked at the door of the farm, and asked if he could buy a glass of milk.

"I can let you have a bottle of yesterday's," said the farmer's wife.
"Oh, thanks," said John. "What time will you be doing today's milking, then?"
"In about ten minutes. You can give me a hand if you like, getting them in."
"I'd love to," said John. "Can I borrow some wellingtons?"

John had a long cool drink of milk, then helped with the milking. The cows walked into a big shed. There were lots of pipes with suckers on.

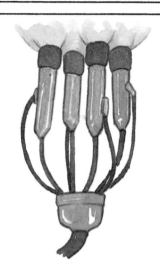

They put the suckers on the cows' udders. Then the milk was sucked out of the cows. It went along a thin pipe, into a big glass bottle, then along a larger pipe into a tank.

"Will I be able to taste the new milk?" said John.
"Oh, no," said the farmer's wife, "you can't drink it straight from the cow. It has to go in the milk-tanker to be pasteurised and bottled in town. They make sure it's really good to drink before you get it."
"How did you milk cows before you had all these machines to do it?"
"We can show you, if you like," said the farmer's wife. "My son's just going to milk one by hand."

She took John out into the yard. There was a cow in a place by itself. It had just had a calf. A young man sat on a little stool. He put a clean milk-bucket under the cow. Then he pulled on the cow's udders, and the milk came squirting out, into the bucket.

"It looks hard work," said John.

"It *is* hard work," said the farmer's wife.

Rosie and Jim hid behind a bale of hay, and watched.

"Well, I never," said Rosie. "So that's how you get milk."

"We get it from the shop, in a bottle," said Jim.

"Look out," said the farmer's wife, "here comes the tanker."
The big milk-tanker came into the yard. The driver pumped the fresh milk into his tanker.

"I'm thirsty," said Jim. "I hope *we* can get a drink of milk."
Then Rosie heard the farmer's wife saying:
"Look he's gone off and forgotten his bottles of milk, and he's paid for them, too!"
"Quick, Jim," said Rosie, "get fizzgog's milk."
So they nipped in and picked up John's bottles of milk.

They were back at the boat long before John. Before he came, they made some fresh milk-shakes. They gave one to Duck, had one each for themselves, and put the rest in the fridge for John. What a surprise he had, when he found them.

John had another good drink, and then it was time for him to write his story about Rosie and Jim and what they would have done today if they had been able to come to life.

This is the story that John wrote in his book.

One cloudy day, Rosie and Jim went for a walk.
"I'm thirsty," said Rosie.
They saw a duck, drinking from the river.
"We can't drink that," said Jim.

They saw a bee drinking from a flower.
"We can't drink that," said Rosie.

They saw a cow, drinking from its trough.
"We can't drink that," said Jim.

"No we can't," said Rosie.
"It's got little fizzly things walking on it.
Where *can* we have a drink?"

"You can have a drink if you jump over the moon," said the cow.
"Jump over the moon?" said Rosie. "Are you mad?"
"Haven't you heard the rhyme?" said the cow. "Everybody knows it."
"Oh yes," said Jim. "*The little dog laughed to see such fun...*"
"*And the cow jumped over the moon,* but the moon's too high for jumping over," said Rosie. "Look, there it is, up in the sky."
"And there's no milk there," said Jim.

"Watch," said the cow.
She took a run at the trough of water, and jumped right over it!

"Look!" said Rosie.
There was the moon, shining in the water of the trough.
"Like a mirror," said Jim.
"So the cow *has* jumped over the moon," said Rosie.

"Clever cow," said Jim. "But where is our drink?"
"Follow me," said the cow, trotting down the lane.
And she led them to the door of the farm.
"Knock twice and ask for the farmer's wife," said the cow, walking
back to the field. "Her name is Janet."

Rosie knocked at the door, and asked for some milk. The farmer's wife had lots of bottles of milk, in her fridge.

Rosie and Jim drank a bottle each, and asked for three more bottles to take back to the boat for John. They paid the farmer's wife and said goodbye.

"Mmmmmmmm...lovely," said Rosie. "Thank you, Janet."

"Delicious..." said Jim. "But it came from the cow before it was in the bottles."

"Thank you, cow," said Rosie. "That was super-fizzy. Goodbye."